W9-BAG-410

Gakky Two-Feet

by **Micky Dolenz** illustrated by **David Clark**

G. P. Putnam's Sons

JP
DOL

To my children, Ami, Charlotte, Emily and Georgia,
and to my good-luck charm, my wife, Donna.—M. D.

To Betsy, who can see over the tall grass.—D. C.

G. P. PUTNAM'S SONS
A division of Penguin Young Readers Group.
Published by The Penguin Group.
Penguin Group (USA) Inc., 375 Hudson Street, New York, NY 10014, U.S.A.
Penguin Group (Canada), 90 Eglinton Avenue East, Suite 700, Toronto, Ontario, Canada M4P 2Y3
(a division of Pearson Penguin Canada Inc.).
Penguin Books Ltd, 80 Strand, London WC2R 0RL, England.
Penguin Ireland, 25 St. Stephen's Green, Dublin 2, Ireland (a division of Penguin Books Ltd.).
Penguin Group (Australia), 250 Camberwell Road, Camberwell, Victoria 3124, Australia (a division of Pearson Australia Group Pty Ltd).
Penguin Books India Pvt Ltd, 11 Community Centre, Panchsheel Park, New Delhi – 110 017, India.
Penguin Group (NZ), Cnr Airborne and Rosedale Roads, Albany, Auckland 1310, New Zealand (a division of Pearson New Zealand Ltd).
Penguin Books (South Africa) (Pty) Ltd, 24 Sturdee Avenue, Rosebank, Johannesburg 2196, South Africa.
Penguin Books Ltd, Registered Offices: 80 Strand, London WC2R 0RL, England.

Published simultaneously in Canada. Manufactured in China by South China Printing Co. Ltd.
Design by Cecilia Yung and Katrina Damkoehler. Text set in Kosmik. The art was done in watercolor and ink on Arches Aquarella paper.

Library of Congress Cataloging-in-Publication Data
Dolenz, Micky. Gakky Two-Feet / by Micky Dolenz ; illustrated by David Clark.   p. cm.
Summary: Although the other hominidees tease him, Gak prefers to walk on two legs instead of four,
and one day his difference turns out to be helpful, just as his mother said it would.
[1. Individuality—Fiction. 2. Prehistoric peoples—Fiction. 3. Teasing—Fiction.]
I. Clark, David (David Lynn), 1960– ill. II. Title.
PZ7.D7022Gak 2006   [Fic]—dc22   2005025176

ISBN 0-399-24468-9
1   3   5   7   9   10   8   6   4   2
First Impression

Since my first visit as a child to the La Brea Tar Pits here in Los Angeles, California, I have been fascinated with anthropology, the study of human beings and their ancestors. That fascination continued through college and exists to this day.

I have often amused myself by imagining what it was like when our ancestors first discovered how to make a fire or realized that they could fashion a tool from a bit of rock, or, in the case of *Gakky Two-Feet*, when they started walking on two feet instead of four.

Current paleoanthropological theory holds that our ancestors adapted to upright walking about four million years ago (around the time of *Australopithecus afarensis*—the infamous "Lucy"). Bipedalism was advantageous to these early hominids as it enabled them to see farther and, hopefully, avoid predators, and it also freed up their hands for other uses, such as food gathering and defense.

Hence, *Gakky Two-Feet*, my first foray into the world of "anthromythology."

We will, of course, never know exactly *what* happened during these defining moments in the course of human evolution, only that they certainly *did* happen. And, who knows? It might actually have happened in precisely this way!

I hope that *Gakky Two-Feet* is as illuminating as it is entertaining.

—Micky Dolenz
Los Angeles, California

Once upon a time, about five million years ago, in a place we now call Africa, there lived a fuzzy little fellow named Gak.

Gak belonged to a group of creatures called hominidees and they lived in a place called Big Trees.

They all liked to eat berries and bugs, swing in the trees, eat berries and bugs, run along the ground, eat berries and bugs, swim in the water and . . . eat berries and bugs.

Gak was just like everyone else except for one thing. . . .
He liked to walk around on *two* feet instead of four.

His friends made fun of Gak and thought he was out of his
silly little hominidee mind. They even had a nickname for him . . .
Gakky Two-Feet.

"Why do you walk around on two feet?" asked Gak's best friend,
Plop. "It's embarrassing."

Gak looked down at his two fuzzy feet and his legs, which were
straighter than his friend's. Then he replied, "I don't know, Plop.
It just feels better."

"Why do I walk on two feet?" Gak asked his mother.

"I don't know, Gak," she said. "You've walked that way since you were tiny."

"But everyone laughs at me and calls me 'Gakky Two-Feet,'" he complained.

"It doesn't matter, darling," his mother said as she picked a big fat juicy bug out of his hair and ate it. "You should never be ashamed of being different. Someday that difference might turn out to be very helpful."

"I doubt that," Gak mumbled.

"In fact," his mother continued, "you can be helpful right now.
These branches keep getting in the way. Why don't you take them down
to the river?"

One day, when Gak and his friends were playing in Big Trees, a cheeky little hominidee named Frizz dared everyone to go out into Tall Grass.

Tall Grass was a huge place next to Big Trees and it spread out as far as the eye could see.

"We aren't allowed to go out there," warned Gak.

"Gakky Two-Feet's a scaredy-cat," said Frizz.

"I am not!" said Gak. "But I am scared of *big* cats—the kind that live out in Tall Grass and would have us for lunch if they could."

"Well, *I'm* going, and anybody who isn't a scaredy-cat better come along with me," said Frizz.

Nobody wanted to be called a scaredy-cat, so they all
followed Frizz.

"I can't see a thing," whispered Plop to Gak.

Gleeb, a pretty little girl hominidee, was limping along beside Gak.
She had fallen out of a tree when she was a baby and had broken her
leg. She had walked with a limp ever since.

"I have a bad feeling about this," she said as she tried to keep up.

Suddenly Frizz stopped in his tracks.

"What is it?" asked Gak nervously.

"I don't know," replied Frizz. "But it sounds like it's big and it's coming this way."

"I knew we shouldn't have come here," said Gleeb.

"What are we going to do?" cried Plop. "If we start running back to Big Trees, it will hear us!"

Just then they heard a loud roar.

"It's a lion! We have to run!" Frizz yelled. And he
took off, without even a look back at his friends.

As quietly as they could, all the others scampered
off in every direction and were soon lost.

As Gak started to run, he heard a voice. "Help!" it cried. He turned and saw Gleeb limping as fast as she could. He didn't know what to do. If he didn't run, he might not make it back to the safety of Big Trees. But if he left her there, she would certainly become lunch for the hungry lion.

Suddenly Gak had an idea! He ran over to Gleeb and scooped her up into his arms like he'd done with the dry branches. Then he stood up tall on his two feet and looked out over Tall Grass.

It worked! He could see everything! The sky, the mountains, and . . . the lion!

But now Gak had an advantage. He could see the lion, but the lion couldn't see him! Slowly, and quietly, he started to back away from the huge beast. Then, looking over his shoulder, he saw Big Trees in the distance.

"Are we safe yet?" whispered Gleeb.

"Almost," replied Gak.

But Gak had spoken too soon. The wind changed direction and the lion got a big whiff of nice, fresh little hominidees. The huge beast turned and headed straight for them!

"It can smell us!" exclaimed Gleeb.

"Yeah, I wish I'd taken a bath this morning," Gak said.

"This is no time for jokes, Gak. Hurry up!"

Gak didn't need to be told twice. And though Gleeb was getting heavy in his arms, he held on tight and ran as quickly and as quietly as he could.

When Gak reached the edge of Tall Grass, he turned and yelled to his lost friends, "This way, everybody!" He ran toward the nearest Big Tree, and his friends followed the sound of his voice.

But the lion also heard him!

Gak could feel hot, hungry lion breath on his back.
The lion leaped at Gak!
Gak and Gleeb leaped up into a tree!
The lion's mighty paw just missed Gak and Gleeb
as they scrambled up into the safety of the branches.

By following Gak's voice, all the other hominidees
had also made it to Big Trees. They sat in the branches,
looking down at the hungry lion.

"You can forget about lunch now, you mangy old cat!"
yelled Plop.

Gak and Gleeb sat together, watching the lion circling below. Gleeb took Gak's hand in hers.

"You saved me, Gak," she said.

Gak turned and shrugged. "Oh, it was nothing."

"I think it was definitely something," she said, and gave him a big kiss on the cheek.

Gak felt his face get hot, and if it hadn't been covered in thick fur, you would have seen it turn a bright red.

When night fell, the hungry lion gave up and disappeared.

Back home, the leader of the hominidees' troop congratulated Gak on his bravery and presented him with an especially big berry. Then he declared that from now on, this day would be remembered as "Gakky Two-Feet Day."

Gak's mother and father beamed with pride as everyone cheered.

"He'll make a fine husband when he grows up,"
Gleeb whispered to one of her girlfriends.

"But what if your children are like Gak and
walk around on two feet?" her friend asked.

Gleeb looked down at Gak and smiled.

Softly, she replied, "That might not be such a
bad thing at all."